TOUGH CHICKS

Written by
Cece Meng

Illustrated by
Melissa Suber

CLARION BOOKS · NEW YORK

Clarion Books
an imprint of Houghton Mifflin Harcourt Publishing Company
215 Park Avenue South, New York, NY 10003
Text copyright © 2009 by Cece Meng
Illustrations copyright © 2009 by Melissa Suber

The illustrations were executed in acrylic.
The text was set in 21-point Cochin.

www.clarionbooks.com

Printed in Singapore

Library of Congress Cataloging-in-Publication Data

Meng, Cece.
  Tough chicks / by Cece Meng ; illustrated by Melissa Suber.
     p. cm.
Summary: Three independent chicks who dare to be different are reprimanded
by the other barnyard residents for not being quiet and docile, until the smart,
fearless trio takes on a runaway tractor.
  ISBN 978-0-618-82415-1
 [1. Individuality—Fiction. 2. Self-confidence—Fiction. 3. Chickens—Fiction.
4. Animals—Infancy—Fiction. 5. Domestic animals—Fiction.
6. Farm life—Fiction.] I. Suber, Melissa, ill. II. Title.
  PZ7.M5268To 2009
  [E]—dc22
2007036837

TWP   10   9   8   7   6   5   4   3   2   1

From the moment Mama Hen's eggs burst open, she knew she was dealing with some pretty tough chicks.

Penny, Polly, and Molly
shook out their wet fluff
and immediately began
to strut around the farm.

Peep, peep, zoom, zip, cheep.

They wrestled the worms.

They raced the bugs.

They dove off the fence
after the pesky barn flies.

"Make them be good!" clucked the hens in the henhouse.
Mama Hen ruffled her feathers. "They *are* good!" she replied.
Though, at times, the chicks did make trouble.

Peep, peep, zoom, zip, cheep.

Penny liked to grab the cow's tail to hitch a ride.

Polly was fond of rooster roping.

And Molly was partial to mud. Lots of mud. She loved a good roll in the pigpen.

"Make them be good!"
called the animals.
"They *are* good!"
Mama Hen clucked.
But sometimes even
she worried.

Like the time Farmer Fred found the chicks looking under the hood of his tractor.

"We didn't touch anything. We just wanted to see how it worked," peeped Penny, Polly, and Molly.

10

"Make them be good," grumbled the farmer. "Chicks don't belong in tractors."

Mama Hen looked at the other chicks.
Some were preening their first feathers
under the morning sun.

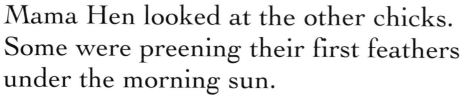

Others were quietly
pecking grain from
the henhouse floor.

Two were hiding under their mama's wing, afraid to come out.
"My chicks are different, all right," thought Mama Hen.
"But they're tough and they're smart and they're different in a *good* way."

Peep, peep, zoom, zip, cheeeeeep.

"Watch out below!" Penny hollered as she swung off the cow's tail and into the yard. The other chicks ran for cover.

"Careful!" Mama Hen
called to Penny.

"Nice form,"
she added quietly.

The hens in the henhouse decided
it was time to teach Penny, Polly,
and Molly how to behave like
proper chickens. They tried to
show the chicks the fine art
of scratching for grain.

Not a speck of grain was found.

The rooster tried showing the chicks how to cluck in a calm and collected manner.

Not a proper cluck was heard.

The pigs even demonstrated how to make a nest.

Not a single
nest was built.

18

When Farmer Fred found the chicks looking under the hood of his tractor again, it was the last straw. He leaned forward and fixed the chicks with a stern eye.

"You are little fuzzy-headed chicks. Be cute. Be quiet. Be good. And stay away from my tractor. I have hay to move before the rain comes."

The chicks watched from the yard as
Farmer Fred drove the tractor around the field,
gathering the hay.

But on his way back to the barn,
the tractor spit out a puff of black smoke,
gave a loud CLUNK, then a long SCREECH,
and came to a sudden stop.

Farmer Fred looked under the hood.
He looked up at the dark clouds.
He looked worried.

Then he walked to the back of the tractor and gave it a mighty push. The tractor began to roll. Faster and faster, it rolled down the hill. It was heading straight for the henhouse.

"BAAAAAAAD IDEA!" bleated the sheep.

"MOOOOOOOVE!"
bellowed the cow.

"WHAT ARE
WE GOING TO
DOOOOOOO?"
crowed the rooster.

While the rest of the animals ran
for safety, Penny, Polly, and Molly
sprang into action.

Peep, peep, zoom, zip, cheep!

They swung off the cow's tail and onto the tractor's steering wheel, turning the tractor in the nick of time.

The henhouse was saved. But the tractor came
to a stop smack in the middle of the pigs' favorite
mud hole.

Mama Hen rounded up her chicks. "I think it's time
we showed these animals how good it is to have tough,
smart chicks around."

The chickens quickly scratched out a plan . . .

26

. . . and the animals went to work.

Under the hood of the tractor, the chicks
tightened belts, checked fluids,
and patched a few holes with Molly's
super-strong mud mixture.

When they were done, Farmer Fred started his tractor.
It worked! The animals cheered.
"Those are some tough chicks," the animals said.
"I know," said Mama Hen.

Farmer Fred stopped his tractor.
"Those are some smart chicks," he said.
"I know," said Mama Hen.

She turned to Penny, Polly, and Molly and
gave them each a peck on the cheek.
"These are some *good* chicks," said Mama Hen.
"We know," said Penny, Polly, and Molly.

Peep, peep, zoom, zip, cheep!